TOUGHBOY
AND
SISTER

TOUGHBOY AND SISTER

Kirkpatrick Hill

MARGARET K. MCELDERRY BOOKS
NEW YORK

COLLIER MACMILLAN CANADA
TORONTO

MAXWELL MACMILLAN INTERNATIONAL
PUBLISHING GROUP
NEW YORK   OXFORD   SINGAPORE   SYDNEY

Margaret K. McElderry Books
Macmillan Publishing Company
866 Third Avenue
New York, NY 10022

Collier Macmillan Canada, Inc.
1200 Eglinton Avenue East
Suite 200
Don Mills, Ontario M3C 3N1

First Edition
Printed in the United States of America
10 9 8 7 6 5 4 3 2 1

Library of Congress Cataloging-in-Publication Data
Hill, Kirkpatrick.
Toughboy and Sister/Kirkpatrick Hill.—1st ed.
p. cm.
Summary: The death of their drunken father strands eleven-year-old Toughboy and his younger sister at a remote fishing cabin in the Yukon, where they spend a summer trying to cope with dwindling food supplies and hostile wildlife.
[1. Yukon Territory—Fiction. 2. Survival—Fiction. 3. Brothers and sisters—Fiction.] I. Title.
PZ7.H55735To   1990   [Fic]—dc20   90-31297   CIP   AC
ISBN 0-689-50506-X

For my elegant, generous,
and talented mother,
❖❖ ISABEL MATSON HARPER ❖❖

1

MAMMA DIED IN OCTOBER, JUST BEFORE
the Yukon froze up for the winter. Toughboy and Sister went through the gray weeks
after that without crying, too surprised to
cry. When Mamma went to Tanana to have
the baby, they'd been so happy, and when
she died, they couldn't find a way to believe
it. It didn't seem that it was true.

Toughboy was nearly eleven. He was
small for his age, and very thin. His hair was
black and straight and always too long. His
name was John, like his father, but like most
Athabascan children in the villages along the
Yukon, he was called by his nickname, which
was Toughboy.

1

Sister was small like her brother, and under the black hair that fell forward over her face, her eyes were steady and serious. Her real name was Annie Laurie, from a song her mother knew. But no one called her Annie Laurie, any more than anyone called Toughboy John. She was always called Sister.

After Daddy heard about Mamma and the baby, he got drunk somewhere. He didn't come home for days. The house was full of people who came from other villages for Mamma's potlatch. Daddy hated it when there were too many people around. He'd been raised in a fish camp, and even the tiny village was too crowded for him sometimes, though only a hundred and fifty people lived there.

There were twice that many in the village now, come to bury Mamma. The town seemed crowded and noisy. A lot of people shook Toughboy's and Sister's hands and said they were cousins. Toughboy and Sister had never heard of some of them, and they grew bewildered when the cousins tried to explain whose mother had been whose niece. So they just smiled politely.

There were women crowded around Mamma's little propane stove cooking for all the people. Some people sat there in the house, and some carried food up the hill to the people who were sitting in the community hall, where Mamma was laid out in her coffin.

Toughboy and Sister were shy with all the strangers in their house. Daddy was gone, drunk somewhere, and Mamma was dead, up there at the community hall, while everyone played cards around her and ate and drank. Toughboy and Sister wished everyone would go home. They sat on the edge of their big bed in the corner of the room and listened to the people talk. Sometimes they went into the little storage room where Mamma kept the old wringer washer, and they sort of hid there. All the people in their house, all the talk and noise, almost made them forget that Mamma was dead. Everything was so strange they could hardly think.

One night they lay in their bed, trying to

sleep while some of the women talked around the table. The light from the bare bulb hanging over the table made the women's faces look unrecognizable and frightening. Sister squeezed her eyes shut so she wouldn't see them. But she opened them again when the women began to talk about her and Toughboy.

"What's the old man going to do about them kids?"

"He never said nothing. Been drunk ever since it happened."

Sister knew that it was Daddy they were talking about. She recognized the voice of a big woman from downriver who said she was Mamma's cousin.

"I think Sister had better go to Nella's aunt in Kodiak. Gladys. She'd do all right there. Sister's pretty smart. She would be a help to Gladys. Gladys isn't getting any younger."

Old Natasha laughed unpleasantly. She lived next door and had known Toughboy and Sister all their lives. She knew everything about everybody up and down the river, and most of what she knew didn't please her. "Well, Gladys wouldn't want Toughboy. She's too fussy. Clean, clean, clean."

All the women laughed. Toughboy was all mud and grease and sand in the summer. Sister could feel Toughboy lying stiff next to her. She knew he was awake, but she didn't dare poke him. He might yell at her or something, and then the women would know they were awake and listening.

"I'll take Toughboy." It was that little skinny woman from Galena, Auntie Dina, married to Daddy's nephew. Toughboy and Sister always called him Uncle Rick, though he wasn't really their uncle.

"Huh," said old Natasha. "You got plenty kids already."

"One more don't matter," the woman said. "Toughboy don't get into no trouble, does he? Seems quiet."

The women were silent for a few minutes, drinking tea. Then they began to talk of other things, and Toughboy and Sister knew that the matter was settled.

They had never thought about what would happen when the potlatch was over and the people all went home. They had never thought about how their lives would change with Mamma gone. It couldn't be that they must leave the village. It couldn't be that they would go away from each other. They turned to each other, frightened.

"What'll we do, Toughboy?" Sister whispered, almost crying.

"I don't know," he answered grimly.

The day after the funeral, after most of the people had gone back to Galena and Koyukuk and Nulato and Tanana and all the other villages, Natasha came to talk to Daddy, Toughboy, and Sister. She told them what she and the other women had planned.

Daddy listened to Natasha with surprise. "I don't want to send my kids nowhere. I can take care of my own kids." He stopped a minute as if to decide if he really meant that. "Yeah," he said. "They're big now. They take care of themselves. No trouble. Me and my kids'll do fine. We don't need no help."

Natasha looked hard at their father. Finally she pushed her chair back and walked to the door, pulling on her work gloves. She looked at Toughboy and Sister, who were frozen where they stood, afraid they had heard wrong. They could hardly believe their luck. Daddy would let them stay, stay in their own village, in their own house, with their own things, with him, with each other.

"You better do right by them kids, John Silas," Natasha said, and she slammed the door as she left.

2

IT HAD BEEN ALL RIGHT. THEY MISSED Mamma, but the women in the village helped them a lot. They were kind in a hundred ways. Not the sort of kind that makes you feel guilty or uncomfortable, but the sort of kind that makes you feel good. Danny's mother made them new mukluks that winter, and Natasha made them mittens and new socks. Whenever they were hungry or if Daddy didn't come home and they were too lonesome in the cabin, they could go to another house. There they'd play with the children and eat and sleep if they wanted to.

Sister would dream of Mamma nearly every night, and of the tiny baby that died with Mamma. In her dreams Mamma would be smiling and holding the little baby out for Sister to see. But Sister could never reach them.

This dream made Sister sad, but talking helped. In their village everyone knew Mamma and talked about her. They told Sister and Toughboy stories about her. Sometimes the stories were funny, and sometimes they were about what a good worker she was. In some ways Mamma didn't seem dead at all because everyone knew her. Sister knew that if she went someplace else where no one knew Mamma, it would be like Mamma was really gone.

Old Natasha kept a close eye on them. She was nearly seventy years old, but she worked just like a man. Everyone in the village was a little afraid of her. They said she was a medicine woman. That meant they thought she could do some magic and make sick people well. Or well people sick. Once Sister asked her if she was a medicine woman. Natasha laughed and looked at her out of the corner of her eye.

"Where you heard that?"

"That's what everybody says," Sister answered. Natasha put another piece of birch in the stove and then sat down. "Well, I'm not," she said. "But let them think it," and she jerked her head toward the houses behind her house.

"My daddy's father was a medicine man, though," she said. She told some stories from the old days then, about when her father was a little boy. She told Sister about the first time he'd seen a white man, and about the underground house he'd lived in. Sister loved those old stories, but she sometimes wondered if they were true.

Natasha would come into the house to see if it was clean. She washed clothes for them in her big gas washing machine. If Daddy was drinking, Natasha would get mad.

"Kyuh," she'd say, making a hard Indian sound in her throat. Then she'd spit on the ground to show her disgust. Sometimes Toughboy and Sister lied and made excuses for Daddy if he hadn't been home for a few days. Natasha always knew when they were lying.

But Daddy wasn't drinking so much anymore, and when he wasn't, he cooked beans for them, and every night, nearly, he popped popcorn for them. He talked to them about the things he thought about while he stretched beaver skins or carved out new stretching boards for marten or worked on the carburetor of the snow machine. On the weekends, when there was no school, he would take them with him to check his traps.

Once Natasha caught Toughboy out late at night, playing in the streets with the other boys, and she yanked him home by the arm. She was frowning terribly. "You. You're not going to be running around like that bunch out there. You get home and be with your little sister. Don't ever let me catch you like that, out late. Your mamma was a good woman. She come from good people. You'll do like her." And she slapped him hard to show that she meant what she said.

After that, whenever Toughboy wanted to

do the things some of the bigger boys did, like steal cigarettes or stay out late, he thought about what Natasha said. He wanted people to be proud of him.

3

IN MAY, AS SOON AS THE ICE WAS OFF THE Yukon, Toughboy and Sister and Mamma and Daddy had always gone to fish camp to stay for the whole summer. When the snow melted and the days grew longer, Toughboy and Sister wondered if Daddy would take them to fish camp now that Mamma was dead. But they were afraid to ask him.

Then one bright day in May, Daddy hurried Toughboy and Sister out of bed. He gave Sister a list of things to buy at the store. "We're going tomorrow," he said.

"Yippee!" yelled Toughboy. He worked with Daddy all that day to get their things ready. They packed boxes of food and all the other supplies they'd need at fish camp. Then they carried the boxes to the boat.

When they finally pushed off from the riverbank the next morning, Sister sat at the front of the boat, holding their old husky, Mutt. Toughboy sat in back by Daddy so he could help him switch gas tanks when the motor ran dry.

It was cold on the Yukon in May, and both Toughboy and Sister wished they'd worn their winter parkas like Mamma always made them do. They huddled against the cold in their jeans and thin jackets. Daddy, small and knotted up like the bark on a cottonwood, his face already darkly brown from the spring sun, squinted his black eyes at the river, not seeming to feel the cold. He was reading the water, keeping a sharp lookout for driftwood so it didn't foul the kicker, the boat's motor.

Toughboy and Sister were happy to be going to fish camp. It was wonderful there—quiet, peaceful, so far away from anyone. There were gulls and camp robbers and ravens, squirrels and weasels. Toughboy and

Sister fed them all. After a few weeks the camp robbers would eat from their hands, and sometimes the weasels would too.

With the bow of the boat Daddy would push the fish wheel out to its place on the river. They would all work hard to get it in just the right place, tied to the bank with strong cable and held in position by a pole. Then every day Daddy and Toughboy and Sister would go with the boat to check the fish wheel. They'd take four or five old wash-tubs to carry the fish.

When the king salmon started to run, they would bring home every day a whole boatful of fish, slithering out of the washtubs, sliding all over the bottom of the boat. Delicious salmon! Enough for the year. Toughboy and Sister were hungry for fresh salmon.

All the other years, that's the way it had been. After Daddy brought the fish to camp, Mamma and Daddy would put on their fish-cutting clothes, and they'd go to the cutting raft. Toughboy would scuttle up and down the bank, fetching buckets of water and bags of salt and whatever else he was told to bring. Mamma and Daddy would work fast, their knives flashing in the sun. Soon there would be a hundred fish or more gutted and hanging on the spruce-pole racks to dry.

Toughboy and Daddy would get the smokehouse ready then. They would bring big chunks of cottonwood to the pit. When the fish had dried enough so that it had a shiny glaze, Mamma would cut the fish into thin strips. Next, she'd soak them in salt-water brine, and then Sister and Toughboy would carry pails of the strips to Daddy. Standing high on the tall ladder, he would hang them in the smokehouse.

Then he would set the cottonwood on fire so that it would smoke just enough to give the fish the perfect smoky taste. And those would be fish strips, better than anything in the world, and Daddy sold them for lots of money. Everyone liked Mamma and Daddy's salmon strips because they were not too dry and not too oily and not too salty. They were just right.

And when they had enough strips,

Mamma would start cutting *kiyoga,* half-dried fish. It was very hard to cut kiyoga the right way, with the slashes just so. Mamma did that by herself. Daddy said he wasn't any good at it.

Last of all, late in the summer they would cut the last run of salmon into dog fish, fish that people used to feed their dog teams.

They would always have plenty of fish to eat all winter and plenty to sell. Daddy didn't have a dog team anymore, so he sold all the dog fish, except for the little he saved for Mutt. Mutt had been Daddy's lead dog before Daddy got the snow machine. Sister thought that Mutt was happy not to have to pull a sled anymore. Daddy said Mutt was retired.

But this year would be different. Mamma was dead, and Daddy would have to cut the fish all by himself. Sister wished she were old enough to cut fish like Mamma. She always told Daddy when he looked sad, "Don't worry. I can help you like Mamma did." Then Daddy would put his arm around her shoulder and his eyes would squint up into a sunburst of wrinkles and he would say, "That's my girl." But they both knew she was too little.

4

THEY HAD BEEN ON THE RIVER AN HOUR
or so when they spotted smoke coming from
the chimney at Danovs' fish camp on the
point. Toughboy and Sister were glad when
Daddy turned the boat toward the shore.
They were always happy to visit the Danovs.

In the winter the Danovs lived at Koyukuk, so usually Toughboy and Sister saw
them only in the summer. But the Danovs
had come to Mamma's potlatch last year, all
the way from Koyukuk. Toughboy hoped no
one would say anything about Mamma.

They saw fat Mrs. Danov, Mary Ann, wav-
ing at them from the door of the cabin. She
liked children and always gave them some-

thing good to eat. She made wonderful homemade root beer, and her doughnuts were the best. She said they were so good because she always fried them in bear grease.

Toughboy tied the boat to the driftwood post on the bank while Daddy climbed the steep bank to shake hands with Mary Ann and Sam Danov. Then Sister and Toughboy walked shyly up the bank to shake hands, too. Sam and Daddy sat on the driftwood log by the door of the cabin and lit cigarettes. Mary Ann took Toughboy and Sister into the cabin to drink Kool-Aid.

She opened a package of cookies for them, chattering all the time, asking a dozen questions but never waiting for the answers. Toughboy was hungry and wished he could eat all the cookies himself. Then he remembered what Mamma had said about being greedy, and he took only three.

After a while Sam came into the cabin and reached behind the door into a box for two beers, which he took outside to Daddy. Toughboy and Sister looked at each other nervously. They didn't want Daddy to start drinking, or they might never get to their fish camp.

Mary Ann saw them look at each other. She pinched her mouth together to show what she thought of the beer. Then she slammed out the screen door and stood looking at Sam and Daddy with her hands on her hips.

"You guys not going to drink no more beer after that one. You got kids with you, John, and you're not going on that river drunk."

"She talks real bossy," Sister whispered anxiously to Toughboy. She didn't know if Daddy would get mad at Mary Ann or not, but Daddy and Sam acted kind of scared of her. They shook their heads to show that they'd never meant to do such a thing. "Just one beer, for chrissakes," said Sam. Mary Ann slammed back in through the screen door and made Sister and Toughboy take three more cookies. Then Daddy came to the screen door and said they had to be going.

Toughboy and Sister thanked Mary Ann

for the cookies and Kool-Aid and then walked down the bank to the boat.

"Them kids don't have enough clothes on, John," Mary Ann hollered at their dad, who was already in the boat. "It's cold on that river this time of year. You better let me give them some blankets."

Daddy frowned, and Sister spoke up quickly, though she truly had been cold. "No, we're not cold. Honest." Daddy could get into an argument just like that lately, and he didn't like anyone talking to him about his kids, telling him how to do things.

Toughboy was afraid, too. He untied the boat as quickly as he could and pushed it out into the current. Then he jumped lightly into the bow while Daddy was still pulling the rope to start the kicker. Toughboy knew he wasn't supposed to push the boat out until Daddy already had the kicker going. He just forgot. He hoped Daddy wouldn't yell at him in front of the Danovs. But Daddy didn't seem to notice his mistake, and the kicker started on the second pull, anyway.

Toughboy and Sister waved good-bye. Mary Ann and Sam Danov stood watching them for a long time with their hands shading their eyes from the sun.

5

IT WAS AFTER LUNCH WHEN THEY FI-
nally got to their camp, which was up a wide
slough that fed into the Yukon. Toughboy
and Sister were glad to be off the river. They
were chilled and stiff and hungry. They
could see that a bear had been there. After
they tied up the boat, they looked at the bear
prints that wandered around the camp. They
saw the claw marks on the smokehouse wall
where he'd tried to find a way in. He hadn't
done much damage. That was lucky. Bears
sometimes broke into the cabins and smoke-
houses of fish camps and tore everything up
for pure meanness, it seemed like.

24

Daddy squatted down with his rifle in his hands to look at the tracks. "Old tracks. Couple weeks old. Looks like a big one."

There were three buildings at their fish camp. The log cabin they lived in had been built long ago by their mother's father. It had a plywood floor and one big window that looked out over the river. Two bunk beds had been built against the wall. Bunched-up mosquito nets hung over the top bunks. There was a fifty-gallon barrel to hold their water, a battered old table with two rickety chairs, and two wooden gas boxes, upended, that served as chairs for Sister and Toughboy.

Lots of things hung on the wall—dishpans and a can opener, saws and other tools, and coils of old rope. There was a long wide shelf over the window and a shorter one over the door.

When Mamma was alive, she would bustle around the first day they moved to fish camp, and somehow she would get things looking right, like home. Sister and Toughboy stood in the cabin door, wondering how they would get the empty, lonely-looking cabin to look right without her.

Hanging by the door was Mamma's fish-cutting apron, old and faded, but Mamma had washed it before they had left the camp last year, so it was clean. Sister felt a hard lump of sadness in her throat when she looked at the apron.

Besides the cabin, there was a tall smokehouse, three times as tall as the cabin, made of old pieces of tin and log slabs and whatever else had been at hand. And behind the cabin was a smaller cabin, sagging with age. Mamma said that her father had built the little cabin first and lived in it until it was too small for his family. Then he had built the cabin they stayed in now. They used the old cabin for a cache, for storage, and there were a million interesting things in there. When it rained, Toughboy and Sister loved to dig around in the boxes and damp to find old things long forgotten.

Down by the water there was a cutting

raft. There the fish were gutted and cut. Daddy would get out the canvas cover for the raft and stretch it across the frame so that they could cut even if it rained or got very hot. On the raft was a long table, and along the bank behind the raft were rows and rows of racks, made out of peeled spruce poles, for drying the dog fish. The bear had knocked down some of the racks, but it wouldn't take much to fix those up.

Daddy brought two of the bigger boxes into the cabin and growled at Toughboy and Sister to help him unload the boat. They scampered out to the bank and helped him pile the boxes and packages from the boat onto the strip of muddy beach. Then, while Daddy and Toughboy carried the boxes up from the bank, Sister started to look through the boxes in the house.

She was looking for the radio. It was so quiet, so strange in the cabin without Mamma. She wanted the radio to fill the room with music from some far-off place where there were a lot of people having a good time. She found it, but when she turned on the switch, she heard nothing but static.

As soon as Daddy came back with another box, she held the radio out to him. "Daddy, please fix it," she wheedled. Daddy grunted but went to the shelf by the window where he found the dusty antenna wires, still connected outside in the big spruce tree. When he fitted the wires to the back of the radio, the sound boomed out into the little room, making them all jump.

What a difference the radio made! Suddenly the little cabin felt pleasant, and the sunshine lying in a square on the floor was welcoming.

6

BUT SOMETHING WAS WRONG. TOUGHBOY
and Sister watched Daddy warily. He was
broody and quiet and looked cross. He was
cutting kindling to start a fire. Sister wanted
to heat water so they could wash up the dusty
table and pots and pans. That was the first
thing Mamma always did. But Daddy suddenly threw down the ax and, without looking at them, said, "I forgot something. I got
to go back to town."

"What you forgot?" asked Toughboy,
quickly. He was hoping he could find it
somewhere, whatever it was. Maybe Daddy
only thought he'd forgotten. Maybe Daddy
wouldn't go back to town.

"Never mind!" Daddy barked at him. "You just get this place straight while I'm gone."

Sister began to cry and ran to Daddy, pressing her face against his shirt sleeve. "Daddy, don't go. I'd get scared to be up here at camp, just us." Daddy smiled a little and squatted down to hold her. He hated to see her cry.

"Gee, be a big kid. You're too big to cry for nothing. Toughboy can take care of everything. And I'll be right back. Just something I got to do."

Daddy took the 30.06 rifle from the corner and hung it on a peg over the door. He nodded at Toughboy to show him that the gun was ready, and then he was gone.

They knew why he had left. He hadn't forgotten anything. He wanted to drink. If he hadn't had that one beer with Sam, he might never have thought about drinking, but now he'd had that one, drinking was on his mind. As far back as they could remember, that's the way it had been. Daddy might go a long time without drinking, and it would be nice and Mamma would be happy. Then someone would come to the house with a six-pack of beer. Daddy would have just one, and that would be the end of that happy time. He would start drinking again and might stay drunk for days.

After ten o'clock that night the sky was still light, as it always is at that time of year in Alaska, and the air was cold. Chunks of ice still floated on the slough in front of the fish camp. Daddy hadn't come back.

Toughboy and Sister sat on the cutting raft and listened hard for the sound of his kicker. They finally went in to bed, too tired to sit up anymore.

7

SISTER MADE TOUGHBOY LEAVE THE
radio on all night so she wouldn't feel so
lonesome. They bundled up in the bunk in
their sleeping bags, and Sister slept hard, not
waking once, but Toughboy was uneasy and
felt like he hadn't slept at all when morning
came.

He was afraid the bear would come back.
He thought the bear would be scared off by
the sound of the radio, so he didn't argue
when Sister insisted on leaving it on. He
knew they were wasting the batteries, but
that was better than having a bear nosing
around.

He thought of what they'd do if a bear

came into the camp. He thought of shooting the bear with Daddy's 30.06, and he felt pretty good the more he thought about it. It would be a real good shot, right in the heart, and Daddy would say, "My boy, he's just eleven, shot a bear the other day up camp."

But then he thought of the time Daddy let him fire that 30.06, and it had knocked him down and hurt his hand where the gun jerked back. He just didn't know if he could hit anything with that big gun. Daddy bought a .22 for Toughboy once. He was pretty good with a .22. Sometimes Daddy would take him out on the road behind town. He'd put beer cans on the twigs of the willows, and Toughboy would shoot at the cans. But Daddy sold that gun when he was short of money, and they just had the 30.06 now. Well, you couldn't shoot a bear with a .22 anyway. Besides, a bear probably wouldn't come around if it heard Mutt barking, so he didn't even need to think about it.

But he couldn't help thinking about bears, somehow. Maybe they could climb way up to the top of the smokehouse if a bear came.

Black bears couldn't climb way up there. At least he didn't think so. He hoped Mutt wouldn't run away from the camp. Maybe they'd better tie him up to be sure.

In the morning the cabin was cold. Toughboy gathered the kindling Daddy had left by the cutting block and a few sticks of pole wood left from last summer.

He had a hard time with the fire. Mamma hardly ever let him make fires. She had been impatient with him because he was slow at it.

He finally got it going with a torn-up box and some birch bark for tinder. He just needed a little practice, that was all.

Then he mixed some biscuit mix with water. That was how you made bannocks. Toughboy didn't know how to cook much of anything, but bannocks were easy. You just fried them on the skillet until they were brown on both sides.

The cabin was still cold, and Sister huddled up close to the stove while Toughboy fried the bannocks. He put water in the kettle to boil for cocoa, too. After they ate their bannocks with butter and drank the hot cocoa, they felt much more cheerful than they had before.

"Daddy probably stayed overnight at Sam and Mary Ann's. Probably he was drinking there with Sam. He'll be home in a little while," Toughboy said.

Sister looked doubtful. "I don't know. Mary Ann would have got mad if he went there. She told them they couldn't drink no more. I think he went all the way back to town."

Toughboy figured she might be right, now that he thought about it, but he said, "Well, anyway, he'll be back today, and he'll have jelly beans."

Sister smiled. Lots of times when Daddy had been drinking, he'd bring them each a bag of jelly beans when he came home so they wouldn't be mad at him.

Toughboy went to the river with a bucket and brought back water to heat on the stove for washing dishes. Sister stood on a chair and took the two dusty dishpans down off their nails and set them on the table. She'd wash the dishes the way Mamma had always done it. But first she got down the tin wash-basin and washed herself and combed her hair and tied it back with plastic barrettes.

She wanted Toughboy to wash up, too, but there was no use in saying anything. He never washed much since Mamma died, and Daddy never thought about telling him to. Danny's mother or Natasha or some of the women would catch hold of him sometimes and march him to a washbasin. But Sister liked to be clean, and she could even wash her own hair if Toughboy helped her get out the soap.

Mamma had washed Sister's hair every week and had brushed it out slowly with an old pink brush she'd had ever since Sister could remember. She would smooth it with her rough hand and admire how it shone in the sunlight. Then she would braid it neatly and so tightly that Sister's eyes were pulled up at the corners. Sister couldn't braid her own hair, so it hadn't been in braids for a long time now.

While Sister did the little bit of dishes and

washed off the table and the windowsills, Toughboy looked for a length of chain to tie the dog. He was afraid Mutt would go off exploring in the woods. Toughboy wanted Mutt right there in camp in case the bear came back again. If a bear came, at least Mutt would bark and warn them.

By lunchtime they had used up all the wood they had. Toughboy began to think about cutting some more. There were two swede saws hanging on the cabin wall. One was nearly four feet long, too big for them to handle, but the smaller one was just right and had a new blade. Daddy's ax was outside, and he'd just sharpened it. They could use that for limbing trees.

Daddy always said the best thing about their fish camp was that there was a lot of firewood nearby. Right behind the cabin, just past a stand of birch trees, was a place where a fire had been. It must have burned a long time ago, even before Grandpa built the cabin. There were hundreds of dead spruce trees standing there, dry and perfect for stove wood. Sometimes you didn't even have to chop them down. You could just lean on them, and they'd fall over. Sister and Toughboy walked to the burn and knocked over three trees. They sawed them up with the little swede saw into stove lengths. Then they brought the wood back to the cabin and stacked it up by the stove. After Toughboy cut one of the pieces into kindling with the ax, they were finished. They felt very proud of themselves and couldn't wait until Daddy could see what they had done.

After that Toughboy made peanut butter and jam sandwiches with the leftover bannocks. He and Sister sat in the cabin eating, listening to the radio and admiring their woodpile. When the sun came out suddenly from behind a cloud, they decided to take their lunch down to the cutting raft.

It was warm on the raft, the first warm day of the year. The sun was hot, so hot they nearly forgot Daddy wasn't there. It was so hot that they felt as if they would never be cold again. The sun pushed through their skins and down into their bones. They were almost asleep when they heard the sound of Daddy's engine.

The boat was just entering the slough, from the sound of it, but Daddy was going very slowly, and the engine sounded sluggish.

Toughboy was worried. "It sounds like something's wrong with the kicker," he said.

Sister looked at him anxiously. They were both afraid that Daddy would be drunk when he got to camp. They stared toward the mouth of the slough, their fingers tight on the railings of the cutting raft, waiting.

8

AT LAST THEY COULD SEE THE BOAT. IT was weaving crookedly down the slough, coming toward the camp. Toughboy held his breath, afraid Daddy would go aground on the sandbar. They looked at each other. He was drunk all right.

Daddy turned toward their landing, but he shut off the kicker before he touched the bank, and Toughboy had to wade out and grab the rope on the bow quickly before the boat drifted downstream. Daddy stood up in the boat and then fell backward, sprawling across the old boat chair and the gas cans.

Sister screamed, afraid he'd hurt himself, but Daddy sat up again and smiled at them.

"Jelly beans!" he shouted, gesturing toward the bow, where he always carried things.

Toughboy tried to help Daddy out of the boat, but Daddy waved him away. He was going to sleep in the sunshine. Daddy lay face down on the hot boards on the bottom of the boat and was asleep in seconds.

Toughboy got the jelly beans out of the bow and returned to Sister on the raft. They grinned at each other as they opened the bags. They felt fine now, knowing Daddy was home.

They ate pilot crackers and jam for supper that night. They weren't very hungry after all those jelly beans. When the fire went out, they crawled into their sleeping bags and went to sleep. This time they turned the radio off.

Daddy was still asleep when they awoke in the morning. Toughboy started a fire and fried some more bannocks and made cocoa. Then they just waited for Daddy to wake up. It was about noontime when they began to see that something was wrong.

Dark, rain-drenched clouds covered the

sun. They walked down to the cutting raft. A cold wind blew on them as they looked down into Daddy's boat.

When she was little, Sister used to stare at people sleeping and try to scare herself. "He's not breathing," she would say to herself while she watched Mutt or Toughboy or one of the dogs. She would stare and stare and stare, pretending that they were dead, trying to imagine what dead would look like and feel like. Then when she was nearly wild, half believing it was true, she would touch them and they would move and the game would be over.

They began to stare at Daddy now, and it was the same as when she'd been little.

"He's not moving," said Sister finally. "He looks dead."

"Don't be so stupid," said Toughboy, and he said it so angrily she knew he was afraid, too.

They watched and watched, waiting for a movement, afraid to touch him. They watched most of the afternoon. It started to rain. Daddy's hair and clothes got wet, and still he didn't move. When the sun came out again, the flies landed on the back of Daddy's shirt and his outstretched hands, and they knew he was dead.

They sat on the cutting raft for a long time as the deck of the raft dried in the sun. They didn't say anything.

Sister's head was spinning with faces. Mamma's, Natasha's, the priest's, and they were all saying to Daddy, "John, you'll kill yourself. John, you're killing yourself. Alcohol will kill you, you'll see. John, you got to lay off that booze." She saw Mamma's face, her eyes screwed up tight with anger. "You'll drink yourself to your grave!"

Finally Toughboy stood up, slowly, stiffly. "I got to make a fire," he said. Sister followed him to the cabin, and after Toughboy made the fire, she huddled next to the stove, staring out the window.

Toughboy spoke to her sharply. "Put water in the kettle. We need something hot to eat." Mamma always said that. Something hot to eat. Sister could never figure out why hot things were better to eat than cold things.

Toughboy looked worried. "Do you know how to cook beans?" he asked her.

Sister thought. "Well, it takes a long time, I know. Mamma used to cook them all day."

Toughboy looked around at the boxes of groceries for an idea. "Let's have eggs, okay?"

He took the skillet off its nail on the wall, wiped out some of the dust with a dishrag, and set it on the stove to heat. He tapped an egg against the edge of the skillet, but the eggshell didn't break. He hit it again, and this time the egg and shell fell into the pan. He fished the eggshell out of the pan and then moved the skillet over to the hottest part of the stove. He'd forgotten to put any grease in the pan, so the eggs stuck. When they were cooked, they were tough and full of big holes because the stove was too hot. But Toughboy and Sister ate them anyway and drank two cups of cocoa each. Then Toughboy put water into the big pan, and they sat down to wait for it to get hot so they could do the dishes.

Sister was afraid to talk to Toughboy because he was upset. When he was upset, he always yelled at her. But after a while she couldn't help but ask him.

"Toughboy, will they send us away now? Like they were going to do when Mamma died?" Toughboy looked up, startled. He hadn't thought about what would happen next. He was thinking about how long he'd waited to be old enough to do things with Daddy. Now he was almost old enough to go moose hunting, old enough to go trapping at the long trap line, old enough to go to the fish wheel by himself and learn everything he'd been waiting to learn. It was as if Daddy had cheated him, telling him to wait, he'd be old enough soon. Then Daddy was gone, and Toughboy never got to do any of those things.

Sister began to cry. "I don't want to go nowhere without you. I don't want to leave town. I don't want to leave Mutt. They wouldn't let us take Mutt, would they? And we can't leave Mamma." She began to cry harder, thinking of the place on the hill where Mamma and the baby were buried with a birch tree at the foot of the grave. She crept into her sleeping bag and cried until she gave herself the hiccups. Then she fell asleep.

The wind began to howl and scream, and the rain came down hard. Toughboy fell asleep, too, silent tears, itchy, tickling tears, sliding down his nose.

9

IN THE MORNING TOUGHBOY'S HEAD hurt so much he could hardly start the fire. When he had the kindling crackling at last, sounding like it meant business, he sat on the edge of the bunk with his fingertips pressed against his forehead. He watched Sister fill the kettle, looking like she was full of something important.

"We have to go today, Toughboy," she said. "After breakfast we'll tie Mutt in the boat and put all the boxes in. You don't know how to start the kicker, do you?" She was sure he didn't, but she asked just to be sure.

"I know how to start it. That's easy," he

47

said. "I just can't pull the rope hard enough to make it start. It's a hard-starting engine."

"Well, we can float home. We'll float out of the slough and then onto the river and past Danovs'. Someone will see us floating by, and they'll come and get us."

He nodded. He looked out the window at the rain slashing the slough.

"We'll wait a little while until the rain stops, though," he said. They decided to leave all their boxes of food in the cabin. Someone in the village would come back with them to get their things. There wasn't room in the boat for any boxes with Daddy sprawled out like that.

Sister fried some bannocks, and by the time the dishes were done, the rain had stopped. While Sister got together the things they needed, Toughboy walked down to the place where the boat was tied.

Then he saw that the wind and rain had loosened the boat from the stake. Or his knot had slipped. He could see the little boat way down the slough, almost to the bend. Desperately, he waded out into the slough, yelling at the boat to stop. Then he stopped, wailing with frustration. There was simply nothing he could do.

He ran up to the house to tell Sister, and from the cabin window they watched helplessly as the boat disappeared from their sight.

"Probably I didn't tie that knot right," said Toughboy. He was so disgusted with himself that he really wanted Sister to be mad at him, too. But Sister wasn't upset.

"It doesn't make any difference, Toughboy. The boat will float to town just the same. And when it goes past town, someone will see it. Then they'll think someone's boat got untied, and they'll go after it. And then they'll find Daddy. And then they'll come to get us."

Toughboy looked at his sister closely to see if she thought she was smart. "Yeah," he said. "I already thought of that."

10

LATER THAT DAY SISTER STARTED TO CRY again. Toughboy couldn't stand it when she cried. He looked at her curled up on her bunk so little and thin, and thought about how he had to be grown up and take care of her until someone came to get them. They needed water and food, that was all. And wood.

He suddenly remembered that they hadn't fed Mutt the night before. It was a good thing he remembered because it made Sister stop crying right away. "What should we feed him?" she asked, horrified that she'd forgotten Mutt.

"Maybe there's some old fish still in the

smokehouse," he said. Outside it seemed the rain had turned everything green at once. All the leaves were suddenly out, pale and sticky on the willow branches and misty green on the birches across the slough.

Daddy's big fish wheel was pulled up on the bank of the slough. It wouldn't be turning this year, and there wouldn't be any fish for them or Mutt. Toughboy looked at it longingly. He had been so hungry for salmon.

They searched the floor of the smokehouse and found enough scraps to take to Mutt. Mutt wagged his whole body and jerked on his chain when he saw them coming. Sister found an old coffee can and filled it with water from the slough for him.

Toughboy decided that water was the easiest of his problems to solve. He went to the cabin for the two buckets and the yoke. Sister helped him fill the buckets from the slough. Then she helped him attach the buckets to the yoke. He walked back up the bank, staggering a little under the weight of the buckets. He tipped each bucket into the big drum in the kitchen and went back to the slough for more. He was out of practice, and he was tired out before he'd filled the drum. But it was over half full, and that would last a few days. And, anyway, someone would be along to get them before it was all gone.

They would need more wood, too. So he and Sister went to the wood patch and cut down three spruce poles. Then they sawed them into stove lengths, and it looked like enough wood for a day or two.

Toughboy was feeling very good about the job he was doing. He thought how Daddy would brag about him.

"My kid, he's just eleven, but he took care of his sister all by himself." Then his throat got tight when he remembered that Daddy wouldn't know.

11

THE CABIN WAS A MESS, WITH BOXES HALF
unpacked all over the table and bunks. It was
making Sister nervous to have everything
jumbled up, but Toughboy didn't want her
to unpack the boxes. Someone would be
coming along soon, he said, and then they'd
just have to pack up those groceries again.

So they packed the wood they'd cut, and
then Toughboy showed Sister how to play
tic-tack-toe. He cut the lines into hard-
packed dirt by the cabin door with his jackknife. And all the time they listened,
wondering when they would hear a kicker.

They talked about what they would do if
everyone wanted Toughboy to go to Galena

and Sister to Kodiak. They would ask to stay together, but they knew Auntie Gladys was pretty old and wouldn't want a boy. They didn't know about the relatives in Galena. They had a lot of kids already. Daddy said they couldn't feed their kids, so why did they keep so many sled dogs. That was a long time ago, and Toughboy and Sister didn't know if they still had their dog team or not, but they knew they had even more kids now. Auntie Dina had said she and Uncle Rick would take Toughboy when Mamma died, but maybe they'd changed their minds since then. Or maybe they'd had another baby.

Sister was crying again. "I don't want to go nowhere without you, Toughboy." He got mad at her and told her to stop being a baby. But then he felt bad for yelling at her. He told her that when they were grown-up, they'd have a house together. In Fairbanks. They'd go to the movies every night. They talked about that house for a while, what it would look like and all the fancy gadgets it would have, and they felt better.

When they were grown-up, they could do

anything they wanted to do. That was good to think about when you were just a kid and you were going to have to do something you didn't want to do at all.

By the end of a few more days they had things going smoothly. Toughboy was getting better at the cooking, but no one came, and the cabin was messier than before.

"Listen," Sister said. "When they come to get us, if they can see that we have things nice and took care of ourselves, maybe they'll let us stay at home. Maybe even in our own house!" She got really excited, the more she thought about the possibility. "They would see how grown-up we are."

Toughboy looked at her doubtfully. He wanted them to see how well he had taken care of Sister. He didn't think anyone would let them stay alone in their house, but they would say, "By God, that Toughboy did pretty good. He had a big pile of wood cut, lots of water. He did okay."

"Yeah," he said slowly, thinking of the praise. "Yeah. I'm going to cut a whole bunch of wood now, and you clean everything up.''

Sister was pleased she'd talked him into it. She was born neat, Mamma always said, and she liked to have everything tidy and just so. She unpacked the boxes, and she lined everything up neatly on the shelves. She piled the boxes outside the door. Then she thought that they would need them again in a few days, so she carried them into the cache, where they'd stay dry and clean.

She swept the floor again and made up the bunks neatly so the sleeping bags covered up the old stained mattresses. She wished she had pillowcases for the pillows, and sheets. Mamma always brought sheets and pillowcases to fish camp, but Daddy hadn't remembered.

When everything was put away, she filled the mop bucket with the rinse water from the dishes and mopped the worn plywood floor. It looked kind of streaky when it dried, and she wondered how Mamma had made it come out nice, but she didn't worry about it too much. She looked around the cabin feeling proud. Everything was in its place. She hung up the dish towels neatly and ran out to help Toughboy with the wood.

They spent two days cutting wood until there was a neat pile under the eaves of the house, where it would be out of the rain. They had a big stack in the house by the stove too. They filled up the water barrel, and they turned over the rain barrel and set it under the gutter so it would catch the rain. They were proud of themselves.

They had been eating so much bannock they'd used up almost all of the boxes of biscuit mix. Sister thought they should eat something else, so Toughboy poured some beans into a big pot, and they put that at the back of the stove to cook all day. When the beans were finally soft enough to eat, they were good. Not nearly as good as Mamma's or even Daddy's, but good enough.

They tried to think how many days they had been there, and they counted back, but they weren't sure. They listened to the radio to see what day it was, but the announcer didn't say. They didn't know what day they'd come, anyway. They thought it was about seven days since Daddy's boat had floated down the slough.

Sister didn't want to tell Toughboy because he would yell for sure, but she was worried about her birthday. She was going to be nine some time in the summer, and she might miss her own birthday. Suddenly she was tired of everything.

"Toughboy," she whined. "When will someone come for us?"

"How do I know," he answered. "Don't start being a damned baby."

Sister looked hurt. "I'm telling Daddy you swore," she whispered dramatically. Then she remembered that she couldn't tell on Toughboy. Toughboy remembered that he wanted everyone to say that he took good care of Sister, and he felt ashamed of being mean. He went to sit on the edge of the bed, his eyes on the floor.

Sister thought he looked like Daddy sitting there. Daddy with a hangover. She ran to him and knelt down beside him.

"Let's be friends," she said as she always did when they had a fight.

"Yeah, yeah," he said, sullen but relieved. He was always glad when Sister tried to make up with him.

He looked at her. "I guess nobody found him yet, is why no one came."

"Maybe they forgot us," she said, her eyes big.

"Dummy." He was scornful. "How they going to forget us? Soon as they find Daddy, everyone will be looking for us."

"Maybe they would think we fell out of the boat," she said.

Toughboy's skin felt cold suddenly. "No," he said, angry again. "How could we fall out and Daddy's still in the boat? Don't be stupid." He felt like crying himself now, and that made him angrier than ever.

"Besides," he said, and he felt good again now that he'd thought of it, "they'd come up here to the camp to check. They would come here first thing." He knew that was true, and he felt fine again.

"Toughboy, maybe Daddy isn't in the boat."

"What do you mean, dummy?"

"Maybe something tipped over the boat. A bear or a moose."

That worried him so much that he stopped being mad. He frowned. "But if they found only the boat, they'd still look for us."

"Well, maybe the boat didn't float very far. Maybe somebody on the river found it and just thought somebody lost a boat and took it home. Somebody from another village. Last year Danny's father found that canoe, and he didn't try to find who it belonged to. He just said, 'Ha, ha, somebody upriver left this on the ice, and it came downriver when the ice melted.' But he didn't know that. Not for sure. Maybe somebody just found Daddy's boat and said, 'Goody, now I have a new boat.' "

Toughboy couldn't think of an answer for all the things Sister could think up. But he knew things weren't as simple as they'd seemed to be. Something had gone wrong.

12

AFTER THAT, THEY DIDN'T LOOK UP THE slough or listen for the sound of a kicker. They cut wood and they ate beans for breakfast and lunch and dinner, and when the beans were gone, they cooked some more. Toughboy hauled water from the slough and fed Mutt, and Sister did the dishes and made the beds. But after the chores were finished, there wasn't much else to do, and Sister liked to be busy all the time.

They watched the very last of the geese coming back from the south and remembered how Daddy always shot some in the spring. Mamma would make goose soup then. They talked about all the good things they used to eat at fish camp—whitefish, ling-cod, duck soup. And when the salmon started running, there would be smoked fish, kiyoga, and salmon strips. The grease from the smoked salmon would smear on their faces and chins. Smoked salmon was delicious, the most delicious thing they could think of. Then in the late summer Mamma would pick berries, and she'd make Indian ice cream with berries and fish grease. Sometimes they'd have bear meat. It made them nearly wild to think of all those good things to eat.

Toughboy began to think a lot about their food. He looked around the cabin carefully one day while he was waiting for their supper to finish cooking. He didn't know how much food they would need for sure, but he was beginning to think they might run out before someone came to get them. There wasn't nearly as much food as when Mamma packed them up.

There were about six more five-pound bags of beans and some boxes of macaroni and rice. There was peanut butter—not much—and a big tin of pilot crackers. They usually ate fish all summer from the wheel, so there wasn't any canned meat or tuna. There were four bottles of catsup because Daddy always ate catsup on everything. There was a big burlap sack of potatoes under the table and a box of powdered milk. They had finished up most of the cocoa mix, though.

They had already used most of the biscuit mix making bannocks, but there was a lot of flour and some other stuff for baking left over from last year. He wished he knew how to make bread. He leaned back against the wall and thought of Mamma's bread, cooling on the table. How good it had smelled!

Sister was drawing pictures with the stub of a pencil on the side of the box they kept their clean clothes in. She loved to draw pictures.

"Sister, do you know how to make bread?"

"No," she said, worried to see his face so serious. "I could knead it if you know what to put in it. And I know how to put the dough in the pan. There's some recipes on the flour bag," Sister said. "Maybe we can find a bread recipe."

So they pulled the burlap bag from under the table, and Toughboy ripped it open carefully with his jackknife. They pulled out one of the twenty-five-pound flour sacks, which fell to the floor with a dusty thud.

They examined the bag of flour. "Georgia Delight Pecan Crispies," Toughboy read with some difficulty. "Maple Orange Refrigerator Bars." They turned the bag over, and there on the back was a bread recipe. "Mrs. Alder's Perfect White Bread." They read it carefully, and Sister could suddenly not wait another minute to taste the fresh bread.

"Let's make it now, okay, Toughboy?"

They got out the dented old bowl Mamma used to make bread and the chipped coffee cup she always measured with. They cautiously measured the water and milk and yeast and flour and salt and stirred it all together. They didn't know what one-fourth meant exactly. They argued about how much sugar that was. Sister wanted to put in four cups of sugar, but Toughboy knew that wasn't right. He wished he'd paid more attention in class when they were doing fractions, but he had never been good at math. In the end they just shook a little sugar into the dough and hoped that was right.

When the dough was too stiff to stir, Sister knew it was time to knead it. She put it out on the table like Mamma did, though she forgot to put flour on the table first and the dough got all stuck to the table and to her hands. Mamma kneaded bread without getting it all over herself or having it stick to the table, but Sister's hands were so gummed up she could hardly move them.

She got disgusted and ran down to the slough to wash her hands. After she got back, the kneading was somehow easier, and she managed to get the dough into a sort of ball. She put it back into the bread bowl, and then they waited for it to rise.

They waited and waited. They slowly ate their supper beans, hardly taking their eyes off the bread bowl. It was getting late. The sun was almost behind the hill, and the sky was pink all over. They grew sleepier and sleepier, and still the bread wouldn't rise.

Then Sister remembered that Mamma always covered the bowl with a cloth while the bread was rising. She took a clean towel out of the clothes box and covered the pan. Maybe it needed to be covered before the bread would rise.

"I'm so sleepy, I'm going to lie down until it rises," she told Toughboy, but he was already asleep and didn't hear her.

When they woke in the morning, the bread dough was spilling out of the mixing bowl onto the table. "Oh, no," said Sister. It didn't look right to her. She peeled the clean cloth off the top of the mass of dough. She tried to push the dough into shape and make smooth little round loaves like Mamma did, but the dough was terribly sticky again. When she finally got the dough onto the baking sheet, the loaves were bumpy and clumsy-looking.

"I thought you knew how to do this," Toughboy said as he stared at the odd little loaves. Sister looked at him sadly, and he wished he hadn't said anything.

After Sister finished the breakfast dishes, the loaves looked ready to bake. Sister and Toughboy put the baking sheet on the top of the stove and covered the loaves with the big roasting pan. That was what Mamma did to make an oven on top of the wood stove. Toughboy and Sister waited by the stove anxiously for what seemed like a long time, and when they could smell the good smell of bread baking, they began to think that they'd done it. Sister kept taking the roasting pan off the bread to see if the loaves were brown. Every time she did that she burned her hands. Finally, when the loaves were a little bit brown, she and Toughboy decided to quit baking them and eat them.

"Mamma says you should never cut bread when it's hot," bossed Sister, and so they had to wait some more until the loaves cooled.

While they waited, they carried water from the slough to fill the water barrel. Then Sister cut the biggest loaf with the long bread knife. They ate the whole loaf with jam. It was delicious, even though it was full of big holes and sort of fell apart instead of sticking together like Mamma's bread.

They were prouder of that bread than of anything else they'd done.

13

THEY HAD NEARLY STOPPED WORRYING about bears. Maybe Mutt's smell and his barking were keeping them away. Besides, there was no fish on the racks to attract them.

The mosquitoes were their biggest problem. They had come overnight, it seemed, and were everywhere. They danced crazily around Toughboy and Sister when they went outside. Their legs and arms were covered with mosquito bites, and Sister's face had sores where she'd scratched the bites until they bled. Daddy hadn't packed any bug spray or Buhach, and the old mosquito nets that hung over their beds were full of holes and nearly useless.

At night it was the worst. The cabin was full of mosquitoes. Mosquitoes whined and brushed against their faces and found every bit of bare skin. Toughboy and Sister hid in their sleeping bags, but they were so hot and uncomfortable they couldn't sleep.

One morning Sister remembered something Mamma had told her. "Toughboy, Mamma said that in the old days they didn't have Buhach to burn. They burned white stuff on trees to keep the mosquitoes away."

Toughboy looked at her blankly. "What white stuff?"

"Oh, you know. That hard stuff. Come on. I'll show you." She pulled him out of the cabin, toward the stand of birches. The tallest birch had a hard gray-white shelf fungus growing on it, not too high up. Sister reached up on her tiptoes and pulled on it. It broke off easily.

"Don't look like it would burn, does it," said Toughboy doubtfully.

They carried it back to the cabin, and Sister put the fungus in Mutt's water can.

Toughboy put a match to the fungus, and they stood watching it, swinging their arms this way and that to keep the mosquitoes away. A thin white smoke began to spiral up. They knelt by the can and watched to see if the smoke drove the mosquitoes away.

"I think it works," Sister said gratefully. They picked all the shelf fungus they could find and rummaged through the cache for cans to burn the fungus in. Soon they had small smoke smudges burning all around the camp. They burned a smudge in the house for a half an hour, and then they set the smudge outside so they wouldn't have to breathe the smoke. All the mosquitoes in the cabin were killed, and they slept soundly and comfortably that night.

They had no sooner solved the problem of the mosquitoes when they began to have a problem with the radio. They could hardly hear it anymore, even when they turned it all the way up. They thought the batteries might be wearing out. Worse than that, maybe the radio was going to break down. They

71

couldn't imagine how they could go on without the radio. They turned it on first thing in the morning and reluctantly turned it off at night. They could get dozens of stations, and sometimes they got Russian radio programs. They never felt lonesome when the radio was on. When it was off and they could hear the silence, they felt their aloneness again.

They decided that they should not play it so often. Maybe they should just turn it on at night, and that way maybe it would last until they could go home. But the silence was too heavy, and they had to play it, even though the sound grew weaker and weaker.

"Probably it just needs new batteries," said Toughboy, trying not to seem worried.

"Do you know how to change the batteries?" Sister asked. "I never did it before."

"Jeez, I'm not sure. Daddy always did that. I'm afraid to touch it. Maybe we'll never get it going again."

They looked at the radio solemnly. "I guess I'll try it," Toughboy finally said.

Sister watched while Toughboy took out his pocket knife and unscrewed the screws at the back of the radio. The antenna wires were hooked to those screws. "I just have to get those wires back on there around those screws after we change the batteries. Then I have to screw the screws down tight again." He looked at Sister when he was finished and saw that some of the worry on her face had been replaced by admiration.

"It's not hard," he said, trying to sound as if he knew what he was doing. He used the blade of his knife to lift the lid that covered the batteries. He carefully pried the four batteries out of their places and put them on the table. Sister brought the new batteries from the shelf. There were only four, but that was just enough.

Toughboy slit open the plastic package with his knife and took out the four batteries. He put them one by one into the hole, but he was uneasy. The batteries didn't fit neatly. They were sort of cockeyed, the two little knobs on top touching each other. The old ones had fitted in nice and tight and straight. He looked at Sister, and she was thinking the same thing, he could tell.

She shrugged. "Turn it on," she said.

He pushed the off-on switch. Nothing. Not a sound.

"Maybe you got them in backward," she said. He turned them the other way, back to back. Still nothing. Now he was really worried.

Sister bent and looked closely at the batteries. "There's a plus and minus sign here. Maybe you're supposed to put them like this." She turned the batteries so that the plus sign on the battery was in the same position as the one on the radio.

Toughboy pushed the switch again, and this time there was a loud crash of static. He was so pleased he forgot about being mad at her for figuring out the batteries. He carefully put the cover back on the battery hole and started to reattach the antenna wires.

"This is the really hard part," he told her. "It's especially important that you get the wires just right or it's never going to work. I know just the right way to do it." He glanced at her to make sure that she was properly respectful and wasn't getting any ideas about that plus and minus business. But Sister looked big-eyed and worried. She watched him carefully. As he touched the copper wire to the screw, the music of the Fairbanks station danced out at them. Sister whirled around the room on her tiptoes.

"We did it! We did it!"

14

SISTER MADE TOUGHBOY CHANGE HIS clothes every week, and she changed, too. But now all their clothes were dirty, dirtier than they'd ever been. It was a kind of mean dirt that looked as if it would never go away. After breakfast one day Sister said to Toughboy, "I got to put water in the washtub and wash these clothes. Everything I got on is so dirty it makes my skin feel awful when I put it on in the morning."

Toughboy thought of how many trips he used to take up and down the bank from the slough when Mamma washed, and he groaned. "That's dumb. We don't need to wash nothing."

Sister knew she'd have to talk fast or else he'd get bullheaded, and nothing would change his mind. "Oh, yes we do, John Silas Junior." She sounded just like Mamma yelling at Daddy. "Do you want them to come and get us and say we look like savages?"

Toughboy slammed out the door. That girl was getting so bossy, like she was so big. He looked down at his overalls, stiff and black. They were so heavy that they looked as though they weren't made out of cloth. It was no use. They had to have some clean clothes, but this was the last time. They would put their extra clothes away in the box, clean, and never wear them. When they heard someone coming to get them, they would hurry and put on their clean clothes. Then everyone would say, "Toughboy kept his little sister clean as a whistle." He imagined himself with his clothes neat and his hair combed. He thought what a nice sight they'd make, standing sadly on the bank with their clean clothes and clean, slick hair. Then he thought about how to make it easy.

He jumped up and banged back through

the screen door. Sister was drying the last dish.

"I know what. We could go wash the clothes on the raft, and that way we don't even have to haul water."

Sister saw immediately what a good idea that was. She had liked thinking about herself with the tub and the scrub board and the hot soapsuds on her arms, like Mamma. But this idea would save a lot of work, and Toughboy was happy again. He always liked to think of easier ways to do things. Daddy used to get mad at him and tell him he worked harder trying to do things an easier way than he would if he'd just gotten to work.

They took the scrub board and the soap down to the cutting raft. Then they decided to wash all the clothes they had, even the ones they had on. Toughboy dressed in Daddy's clean pants and shirt rolled up at the cuffs and sleeves. Sister wrapped Mamma's clean fish-cutting apron around her. Then they pulled the box of dirty clothes to the raft.

Sister lay on her belly on the raft and

dipped her shirt in the water. She had to hold on tight so the current wouldn't pull it out of her hands. Then she laid the shirt on the raft and rubbed Fels Naptha soap all over it. She rubbed the soapy shirt up and down on the washboard, and when she thought it was clean enough, she rinsed it in the slough. And that was one thing washed. Toughboy did the same, and before long they were finished with the laundry. They both got very wet, and when the sun went behind a cloud, they began to feel cold. They piled all the clean clothes into the washtub and carried it between them up to the cabin. When they hung the laundry on the clothesline behind the cabin, the line sagged nearly to the ground in the middle, so they used just the high parts at the ends.

It rained for the next three days, so they had to wear the old apron and Daddy's extra clothes until their clean clothes finally dried out. Even then it seemed as if there was a lot of dirt left on those clothes. But Toughboy wasn't worried, and he told Sister that it didn't matter because the dirt was clean dirt.

15

THE DAYS WENT ON, ONE AFTER AN-
other, and they always had the same things
to do. They ate oatmeal every morning, un-
less there were beans left over from the night
before. Then Sister did the dishes, and
Toughboy filled the water barrel. They
would put more beans on to cook, and then
they'd go to the wood patch for a few poles
of wood. They made bread a couple of times
a week, and they were getting better at that.
They washed clothes once a week. But there
was still lots of time left over, and it was hard
to fill all that time.

One day when the sun was hot, Sister
couldn't think of a thing she wanted to do.

She decided to look through the old cache behind the house. Maybe there was something interesting there.

The roof of the cache leaked, and the things in there were musty and damp. She was sure there were spiders and horrible things in the corners. But she remembered there used to be a box of magazines. She wanted something to read so that she could lose herself in pictures and words. She would struggle through the hard words, slowly, until the meaning suddenly burst on her mind.

There was only one window in the cache, so dirty it didn't let in much light. She pulled all the boxes out into the hot sunlight, where she could see. She knelt there on the ground breathing in the secret musty smell and began to open the boxes.

There was a fishnet they'd forgotten about, and a wooden gas box full of beaver snares. She wondered if Daddy knew about the beaver snares. He was always short of traps. She bet he'd forgotten they were there at fish camp. She found boxes of clothes that smelled so old that she couldn't imagine who they had belonged to. In one of the boxes she found a tiny baby dress with little flowers embroidered on the yoke. She wondered if it had been her dress.

In an old suitcase that was back in the farthest corner of the cache she found a large envelope. In it was a picture of some Indian people in old-fashioned clothes. There was a woman with long skirts and a tight jacket, and some children with high laced-up boots. The woman looked a little like Mamma, but her hair was all slicked back. The man in the picture had on a pair of high beaded moccasins, made the way Natasha had said people made them long ago. The year "1903" was written on the back of the photograph. Sister knew that Mamma had thought this picture was lost. She wanted so much to tell Mamma that she'd found it. She wanted to tell Daddy about the beaver snares.

Sister carried the picture to the kitchen and placed it carefully on the shelf.

❖❖❖

The box of magazines was way in the back of the cache, too, so it was nearly supper time when she found it. The box was too heavy for her to carry. She carried the magazines, a few at a time, to the cabin. They were a little damp and limp, so she laid them neatly on the bench near the stove to dry out when she lit the fire to cook supper.

After they'd eaten dinner, Toughboy and she looked through the magazines. They were careful not to tear the damp pages. "Hell," said Toughboy. "These are old." He pointed to a picture. "They don't have no cars like that now. This is the same as Billy Sam's truck, and he said his truck was thirty years old."

Sister only glanced at Toughboy's truck. She was not much interested in such things. She was fascinated by the fat babies and pretty ladies with curly hair and hard red smiles. Most of the words were too difficult, but she was able to read some of them.

"April 14, 1942," said Toughboy. *"Saturday Evening Post.* That's old," he insisted. He saw by the expression on her face that she was not paying attention to him at all, so he went back to looking at the car ads.

Whenever their work was done and there were restless hours to fill, they read those old musty magazines. Sister cut pretty pictures from them and hung the pictures on the wall. She cut out the ladies and their babies and played pretend with them for hours at a time. After a while they seemed like old friends.

16

TOUGHBOY LAY IN HIS BUNK EARLY ONE morning, staring at the shelf of food over the door. When they had first come to camp, the shelf was full, and there was lots more food under the table. Now there were empty spaces on the shelf and nothing left under the table except the big sack of potatoes and half a paper bag of flour.

He knew something had happened, something bad. Maybe no one would ever come to get them. He turned on his side to get away from the bright sun streaming in on his face. Maybe no one would ever come, ever. But when they didn't come back to the village in the fall, someone would know, wouldn't they?

He didn't know how far away fall was. There were no berries yet on the hill where they cut the wood. But some years the berries were there and other years they weren't, so it would be hard to tell by the berries.

Daddy always said you couldn't starve in the woods. And there were lots of fish in the slough, but the fish wouldn't bite close to the bank. One thing for sure, Toughboy wasn't going to talk about this to Sister. She'd just get worried and start to cry.

But as soon as he heard her turning over in her bunk, he leaned down and said to her, "Sister, we got to get some fish."

Sister's voice sounded muffled. Her head was way down in her sleeping bag. "We'd better get out the fishnet, then," she said.

He lay back in the bunk. He'd never thought about that net. "Yeah," he said. "That's what I meant."

After breakfast they pulled out the net from the cache and laid it out on the bank of the slough. It was musty and full of holes.

They dragged it down to the slough and stared at it for a while. They knew it was supposed to be set with a boat, and that you put something that floated at one end of the net to hold it out in the slough. They didn't have a boat, so they tied one end of the net to the fish-cutting raft and tied an empty gas can to the other end of the net. Then they threw the net out into the slough as far as they could. It just drifted with the current.

"It's way too long," said Sister. "Maybe we could cut it short and then put something heavy on the bottom so it won't float away like that."

Toughboy was puzzling over this solution. "Well, how are we going to get the fish out of it, anyway?"

"We'll just put a weight on one end that isn't too heavy for us to pull in," Sister answered reasonably.

So they cut the net shorter and tied the big swede saw to the bottom. They didn't use that big saw, anyway; they used the little saw.

The net was easier to throw out, and it seemed to stay in one place. They watched the net all day. The gas can they used as a float moved a little way down with the current, but not too much.

"Do you think we have any fish yet?"

"Let's wait until after supper to see," said Toughboy.

After supper they lay on their bellies on the raft and slowly pulled the net toward them. When they had pulled it up on the raft and stretched it out, they found it was full of small pieces of driftwood.

It took them a long time to untangle the net again and take out the sticks. Then they threw the net back out again. Toughboy began to worry.

"Maybe the fish just go up the middle of the slough, like they do in the river sometimes. Daddy always had to keep his fish wheel out far. If it got too near the bank, he'd push it out again because it wouldn't catch any fish if he didn't."

That idea made Sister cross. She put her

hands on her hips like Mamma did. "Well, Toughboy, we have to get some fish. We're just about out of food, and now we have to eat those potatoes."

"Oh, don't get excited. We'll get some fish tomorrow. Don't worry," he told her. But he wasn't so sure.

They didn't get any fish that day or the next. They were out of beans then and had finished the macaroni, and so they opened the sack of potatoes. Neither of them liked potatoes very much. That's why they'd saved them until last. Sister peeled potatoes for breakfast, but when she finished, they were very small, much smaller than when she'd begun.

"Cripe," complained Toughboy. "You can't take off so much potato with the peelings."

"Well, you try then," she said, pouting. He peeled them because he just didn't have the energy to argue. His potatoes were better, so peeling became his job from then on.

It took a lot of potatoes to fill them up. Worse than that, plain potatoes were a miserable meal.

Toughboy and Sister hadn't minded oatmeal every morning because Mamma had made them oatmeal lots. And she had made beans all the time too. But Mamma had never, never put plain potatoes on a plate for their supper like that. Potatoes all alone, without fish or moose meat or something, made them feel sad and lonely.

Toughboy and Sister didn't have much to feed Mutt, either. They cooked enough potatoes for him too, but at first he just looked at his pan suspiciously and then knocked it over to show Toughboy and Sister what he thought of potatoes. After a few days he began to eat them, though.

Sister worried about Mutt more than anything. "Toughboy, if we turned him loose, he could catch rabbits or shrews and get his own dinner."

"But what if he doesn't stay close to camp. We need him in case of bears."

"We haven't seen any bears all summer,"

said Sister. "Maybe they won't come if we don't have fish in the smokehouse. And Mutt looks just skinny."

"Okay," said Toughboy. But he was worried. He let Mutt loose and immediately Mutt dashed off into the underbrush.

"See, I told you so!" Toughboy hollered at Sister.

"He'll be back," said Sister, but she sat on the step in front of the cabin, anxiously listening to Mutt crashing through the brush. After a while she stood up and called him, and soon Mutt came dashing back to her. He jumped up on her with both front paws and nearly knocked her down. Sister hugged Mutt as if he'd been gone for hours.

"Kissing a stupid dog," said Toughboy.

From then on Mutt got his own dinner.

17

IT BEGAN TO RAIN THAT WEEK, AND IT rained for a long time. It was a cold, hard rain, and they had to stay indoors. The batteries began to get weak again, and they had no more. They tried to keep the radio off except at night, but they couldn't stand the quiet in the cabin. It made them feel so lonesome.

Finally the radio went dead, and the silence was so loud and heavy that Sister thought her heart would break. They sat in the silence for a few minutes, and then Sister ran to Toughboy and put her arms around his neck. She was crying. Toughboy thought of telling her how stupid she was, but he didn't. Instead he ran across the floor and jumped on the bench by the window. He threw his arms wide like a man in the movies. "Once a jolly swagman camped by the billabong," he sang. Sister looked at him and giggled. Toughboy never acted silly or fooled around. And she sure never heard him sing.

" 'Waltzing Matilda,' " he said. "I know all the words to that. We learned it in school last year. It's my favorite song." He was pleased that he'd made Sister smile. He was pleased at how loud he'd sounded in the cabin.

"Sing it then, Toughboy." Sister settled back on her bunk with her knees under her chin.

Toughboy was beginning to feel silly. "Wait till we're in bed," he said.

When supper was over and the chores for the night were done, Sister reminded him about the singing. After they were in their sleeping bags, he sang "Fox Went Out on a Chilly Night" and "From the Halls of Montezuma." There were a lot of songs he remembered from school. He had a very nice voice, and when he sang, the lonesomeness went out of the cabin.

After a few more days the rain stopped, and they went out to check on their net again. They hadn't looked at it since the rain had started. They didn't have any hope this time, but there at the end of the net was a hooknosed salmon. His teeth and snout were tangled in the net. They tried to work him loose, but he squirted out of their grasp. Finally Toughboy had to cut the net away with his pocketknife.

They had a fish.

Sister ran to the cabin to get Mamma's fish-cutting knife. This was a curved blade with a handle that fitted in your palm. In Athabascan it was called a *clabas*. Toughboy knew the first thing to do was to cut off the head of the fish. He hadn't expected it to be so hard to cut. He sawed away on it for a while before it came off, and then Sister carried the head to Mutt's dog pan. It would be a surprise for Mutt when he came back from hunting in the woods.

Toughboy was feeling more confident by

the time Sister got back to the raft. He had slit open the fish's belly the way he'd seen Mamma do it a million times. He forgot about taking the fins off until Sister reminded him, but he said it wasn't important, anyway. Soon they had ten big pieces of salmon.

Sister ran back to the cabin to get a pot, and they decided to boil the fish all at once, all ten pieces. The smell of the boiling fish was wonderful. They forgot to boil potatoes to go with the fish, but that didn't matter.

That fish was the best fish they'd ever tasted. They ate nearly all of it but remembered at the last minute to save some for breakfast. Sister was so full that she could hardly move. She told Toughboy she wouldn't do the dishes that night but would wait till the morning. She crawled into her sleeping bag and was asleep in no time.

18

WHEN SISTER WOKE IN THE MORNING, she heard Mutt whining softly, nervously. She could tell that he was in front of the cabin door. She jumped out of the bunk to let him in, and when she opened the door, she saw what Mutt was whining about.

There on the cutting raft was a black bear. He was eating the scraps of fish they'd left there the day before when they'd cleaned the fish.

"Toughboy," Sister whispered. "Toughboy!" She couldn't move. The bear ambled away up the beach, as she watched, and lumbered into the woods. Mutt stopped whimpering and flew into a rage. Now that the bear was gone, he snarled and barked so savagely and wildly that Toughboy sat straight up in bed.

Toughboy could almost guess from the look on Sister's face what had happened.

When she had finished telling for the fourteenth time exactly what she'd seen, Toughboy looked in disgust at Mutt. "Huh, some bear dog you are!"

Sister defended Mutt hotly. "I think it's a lot smarter not to go out and get all tore up by a bear. Daddy always said it was better if the dogs didn't bark. That way you could get a good shot at the bear."

Toughboy thought about that for a minute. It made sense, he guessed. "We shouldn't have left those fish guts out there." He groaned. "That was just stupid."

"Mamma's clabas!" said Sister, suddenly remembering. "I left that on the raft too. Oh, Toughboy, if he knocked it in the water! Mamma loved that knife."

At the cutting raft, they couldn't find the clabas anywhere. Toughboy drew in his breath sharply.

"Look what he's done to the net." The bear had been in the water with the net, it looked like. When they pulled the net all the way out of the water, they found that it was torn and tangled.

"Why do bears just tear everything up for fun?" asked Sister.

"We sure can't use this net anymore." Just when they thought they would have fish to eat, just when they'd learned to set the net, it was ruined. Toughboy's face was grim. Then he remembered the other half of the net in the cache, and he smiled. "Good thing we cut the net in half, huh."

After breakfast they set the new net, which had even more holes than the other one had had. Their wood supply was low because they hadn't gone out much during the long rainy week. But they were afraid to leave the camp and go to the wood patch.

"We'll take Mutt and tie him up near us while we cut wood. And we'll take the gun," Sister said. So Toughboy slung the heavy rifle on its sling over his shoulder. But first he practiced sighting a few times down the barrel, just pretending to pull the trigger. He knew if he fired it, it would knock him down. But a 30.06 could stop a bear right in its tracks. Nothing to worry about there.

Still they were so nervous in the wood patch that they cut just a few poles and hurried home. They were glad to be back inside when the chores were done, even without the radio.

They read the old magazines again, and Sister cut out more pictures to pretend with. They'd had the last of the fish for breakfast, so it was boiled potatoes again for supper. Toughboy felt cross.

The mosquitoes had been gone for quite a while now, but the gnats had come, and Toughboy hated gnats. He hated them worse than the mosquitoes. That day in the wood patch he'd been bitten all over, and his face was sore and swollen. Gnats never bit Sister much. It wasn't fair. They were burning a smudge in the cabin again because of the gnats, and his throat felt sore and his eyes were stinging.

Toughboy was so bored that he felt like kicking the walls. He was tired of looking at the magazines, and he wasn't sleepy, and he didn't want to go outdoors because of the gnats and because of the bears. He frowned at Sister as she played with her cut-out pieces of paper. She could think of things to do all the time. Pretend, pretend. One of the cut-outs was Dorothy from *The Wizard of Oz,* and she had a sort of lion and two other paper men who were supposed to be the Scarecrow and the Tin Woodman. He remembered that story a little. Miss Denson had read it to them the year before, or maybe it was the year before that. He listened closely and forgot the itching bites on his face. Sister remembered every little detail, like she was reading it from a book.

When she got to the part about the winged monkeys, she stopped suddenly and put all the paper pieces together. How could she stop just when the story was getting good? "Don't stop now," he said crossly. She looked up at him, astonished. He felt a little foolish for making it sound so important.

"I mean, I forget what happens next."

Sister looked at him for a moment. "I'll tell you the rest after I get in bed," she said. She waited for him to sneer at her and tell her he didn't want to hear a stupid kid story. But he just nodded.

When they'd crawled into their sleeping bags, he reminded her to start. In a teacher sort of voice Sister continued the story until she was yawning between every two words. She told Toughboy that they'd have to finish the story the next day. Toughboy could hardly wait.

In the morning they woke up fast, the minute they heard Mutt give his low whine. They hurtled out of their bunks and rushed to the window. The bear was there again, with one paw in the water, raking at their fishnet. They couldn't see around his fat black rump, but it looked as if he was pulling the net out. Toughboy got the gun down. He barely felt its weight.

While Mutt whined softly, the bear nosed around the fish racks and then, just as it had done last time, ambled slowly away out of camp. Mutt broke into a frenzy of barking as soon as the bear was out of sight.

When they went down to the raft, they found their last net in shreds. "I wonder if it had a fish in it," said Sister.

19

THE BEAR CAME BACK NEARLY EVERY night or morning after that. He snooped and prowled. He stood up and raked the tall smokehouse walls with his claws. He turned things over and clambered all over the fish wheel. If he knew they were in the cabin, he didn't show the slightest fear. Or the slightest curiosity. But Toughboy and Sister could hardly sleep anymore at night. They slept during the days sometimes, taking turns.

Toughboy thought Sister's face looked little and thin. There were dark circles under her eyes.

The funny thing was that they weren't quite as afraid of the bear as they had been in the beginning. They watched him carefully when he was in the camp, but they were used to his ways now. He just liked to snoop around the edges of the camp. He was like a troublesome baby or a puppy.

The potatoes were nearly gone. Neither of them talked about what they would do when there were no more left.

Sister told a story to Toughboy every night, and sometimes he got her to tell one during the day when they were in the cabin. It seemed to Sister that she told stories all day long. She told all the ones she could remember from school, and all the movies she'd ever seen at the community hall. She made up some. But when Toughboy knew it was her own made-up story, he would make her change things or give the story a different ending.

Early one morning Toughboy was suddenly startled awake by something. He knew it was the bear when he heard Mutt whine. Toughboy almost didn't want to get out of bed to watch him. Then he heard a sudden change in Mutt's tone.

Toughboy went quickly to the window. He saw the bear coming toward the cabin. The bear came on steadily, as if there was nothing in his way. No cabin at all, only air.

Toughboy stared at the bear, even forgetting that he should get the gun. Mutt was whining crazily now, digging frantically at the door.

Sister was awake. "Mutt!" she whispered. "He'll kill Mutt!" They simply didn't know what to do. It was like a dream, Toughboy thought. You try to run and your feet won't move. Or you try to scream and no sound comes out of your throat.

The bear veered off to go behind the cabin, and they lost sight of him. They could hear him snuffling around outside the cabin. They could almost feel his hot breath coming in through the cracks in the walls. The bear stopped to clean himself, and the loud smacks and slurps he made as he noisily licked his fur were somehow more frightening that a growl. Then they saw his face peering in through the window at them.

They stood stiff, unmoving, looking into his little mean eyes. Then the bear stood on his hind legs and sniffed at the roof. He dropped to all four feet again and disappeared from their sight. In a few minutes they saw him waddling off into the woods.

Mutt still whined at the door, and Sister flew to let him in. There was no fierce barking this time. Mutt crept under the bunk and was still.

Toughboy's knees had suddenly begun to shake. He sat uneasily on a chair at the table trying to get his knees to stop. Sister ran to her bunk and huddled in the sleeping bag, shivering all over.

"Toughboy, those eyes," she said after some time. And then a long while later she said, "Toughboy, could he break the window?"

"Huh," said Toughboy. "He couldn't break no damned window." But he knew he could.

20

AT LAST THE DAY CAME WHEN THE potatoes were all gone. The only food left on the shelf was the big tin of pilot crackers, Daddy's four bottles of catsup, and a few tea bags. They would eat pilot crackers with catsup for breakfast and for dinner. They wouldn't eat anything for lunch anymore.

All that afternoon they picked the blueberries that were growing here and there around their camp. There weren't very many this year, and it took them a long time to get a big bowlful. The following day they would look for more blueberries around the wood patch.

The next morning the bear was back

again. They didn't wake up until he was standing at the window, his brown muzzle pressed against the glass. Toughboy slid out of the bunk and took the gun off its peg.

The bear pushed one paw through the window, and the glass flew across the room to the bunk. Sister began to scream. She screamed and screamed, and then Toughboy shot right through the window. He couldn't see if he'd hit the bear.

The recoil of the gun knocked him down on the floor. His ears hurt from the sound of the shot in the tiny cabin. He got to his feet and looked out the window. The bear was limping away from the cabin. He knew he had to kill the bear. Everyone knew how dangerous a wounded bear was. He cocked the gun and shot again and again. He stood with his feet planted far apart, and the gun didn't knock him down, though it pounded his shoulder like a sledgehammer.

The bear was still crawling, but when Toughboy fired again, there was just a click. No more shells. The gun was empty.

He carefully laid the gun on the table and wiped his upper lip, which was dripping with sweat. Sister was sobbing in her bunk.

He stared at the bear through the broken window, and as he stared, he heard the ravens screaming. The bear had stopped right at the edge of the woods. He was nearly hidden by the underbrush, but Toughboy could see his rump and his hind leg. He was lying still. Toughboy couldn't think. He felt that if he didn't take his eyes off the bear, he could keep it lying there. If he stared hard enough, maybe the bear wouldn't get up again. He didn't pay any attention to Sister's sobbing. He just stared at the bear until his head and his eyes hurt. The ravens were still hollering, all excited by the shots.

After a long time he could feel the pain in his hand and in his shoulder where the gun had hit him. He didn't know how long he'd been watching the bear, but soon he felt Sister's hand on his arm, and they watched together.

Finally she spoke. "Is he dead?"

"I don't know," said Toughboy. He looked at her. "I don't have no more shells." Sister was quiet a moment.

"Probably he's dead," she said.

They relaxed enough to sit in the chairs by the table. For long hours they watched the bear, and he never moved. When they saw a raven land on his body, they knew it was true. The bear was dead.

Then Sister asked Toughboy to make a fire, and she heated a pot of water and made them some tea. It tasted good with the crackers, even if they didn't have any sugar.

··· 21 ···

THE NEXT DAY THEY FOUND A BIG PATCH
of cranberries on the knoll behind the wood
patch. They ran back to the cabin to get a big
pan. All day they picked, keeping Mutt by
their side, and they ate until they were really
full for the first time in a long time. Sister
made sure they had enough berries for
breakfast before they went back to the cabin.

Every morning after breakfast they went
out to pick berries. It was cooler now in the
mornings, and the gnats were not very bad.
One day on their way to the wood patch
Toughboy looked up and saw that one of the
birch trees had a branch of yellow leaves. It
stopped his breath for a minute. Fall. Winter

coming. For sure someone would be there soon.

The days were sunny and beautiful. In the mornings it was chilly, but when Toughboy and Sister got to the berry patch, the berries were sweet and hot in the sun. They were eating so many berries that they didn't need to eat so many pilot crackers. There were still a lot left, and two bottles of catsup. But they were all out of tea, and they had only one box of matches left. Toughboy carried the matches in his shirt pocket so that they wouldn't get lost.

And that was how the terrible thing happened. Sister had been playing on the raft, and she called to Toughboy to see the fish jumping in front of the raft. He had a crazy idea that maybe he could catch a fish with his bare hands. So he bent way over the edge of the raft when the fish jumped again, and the matches slipped out of his pocket into the slough.

They both grabbed for the box so fast that they almost fell into the water, but it was too late. They ran down the bank, wading out as far as they could, trying to reach the box with a stick. The box bobbed like a little boat, carried by the ripples away from them.

They couldn't think of anything to say. Nothing more terrible could have happened. No matches, no fire, no hot water. It was beginning to grow dark at night. Fall had arrived here, and soon it would be so cold. They had done their best, but they were just about beaten now. Someone had to come to get them soon.

They began to listen again. They sat up quickly in the berry patch and told each other, "Listen!" But it would be the wind in the leaves or a bird's wings beating hard against the sky, and they would go back to picking again. And then they would sit on the raft with their knees tucked under their chins, staring out at the bend of the slough, listening.

Sometimes at night when Sister was telling a story, she would suddenly stop, alert, and they would both listen hard with their breath stopped. They weren't really interested in the stories anymore, and so she stopped telling them. They were only interested in listening, listening as hard as they could.

And then one morning, at last, they heard the sound of a kicker coming toward them from far down the slough.

22

IT WASN'T AT ALL AS THEY HAD THOUGHT it would be. The little boat putted up the slough, and they saw right away that it was Natasha's boat. They just stood there, by the cabin, and didn't run down to the raft to help her tie up. They didn't look at each other, and even Mutt just sat by their heels and whined softly.

Natasha's head was wrapped in a scarf, and she had her work clothes on. She carefully tied the boat and hardly looked at them as she walked up the bank toward them.

When she stood in front of them, she looked cross. "Huh," she said, as if things were the way she expected and not at all good. Her dark brown eyes glittered in the sunlight. "Skin and bones," she said, looking them up and down.

Toughboy felt sick inside. He wanted her to notice that he'd taken care of Sister.

"We ran out of food," he said sullenly.

"Oh," Natasha said. "I thought the cat had your tongue."

"We caught a fish, but the bear tore up our net," said Sister. Natasha looked mean as a bear herself.

Suddenly Natasha's face softened. *"Colah,"* she said quietly. Poor things. Toughboy's throat grew tight, and he was suddenly terribly afraid he was going to cry. He turned away quickly and walked to the cabin. Sister had begun to cry softly against Natasha's shirt. Natasha fished a Kleenex out of her hip pocket and gave it to Sister. Then she walked into the cabin.

She looked around critically. "Clean." She nodded briskly. "Neat." Sister smiled proudly.

Natasha turned to Toughboy. "Go down to the boat and get the box in the bow.

Food." Toughboy tried to walk slowly, but he broke into a run going down to the bank. Now he wasn't afraid he was going to cry; he was afraid he was going to giggle. He felt so happy at the thought of food that he was afraid he was going to act stupid.

He lugged the box back to the cabin. Natasha opened the box so slowly that they could hardly bear it. She laid oranges and candy bars and smoked fish on the table. They stared at the food.

"Eat," Natasha said.

While they wolfed down the food, Natasha walked outside and looked at the neat little woodpile. She examined the washtub where their dirty clothes were soaking, ready to wash. She folded her mouth together and shook her head.

Toughboy was wishing that almost anyone had come except Natasha. Someone who would notice how well he'd taken care of Sister.

Natasha walked back into the cabin and took a cigarette out of her shirt pocket. She lit it while they watched the match carefully.

Sister saw that Natasha had noticed the way they looked at the match. "We ran out of matches," she explained. Toughboy was relieved that Sister didn't tell how he'd dropped them in the slough.

Natasha nodded. She took another puff on the cigarette, and then she said carefully, "What happened to your father?

They looked at each other. Then Toughboy told Natasha about the night Daddy had come home from the village. Natasha was silent, smoking.

Finally Sister asked, "You never found him?"

"No," Natasha answered. She thought for a minute. "Maybe caught in a snag. Or swamped. I watched for you all summer. Yesterday I knew something was the matter. John would have had you back for the first day of school."

She looked around the room. "Here all summer by yourselves." Her voice was flat.

"Toughboy shot a bear," said Sister. There was a flicker of interest in Natasha's eyes, but she didn't say anything. She just looked at Toughboy. Then she stood up and tossed her cigarette into the cold wood stove.

"Well, well. So that's how it was." She gestured at the shelves. "Pack up your stuff. Get it all in the boat. We'll go back to town."

Toughboy and Sister didn't move.

"Well?" Natasha asked crossly.

"Toughboy took good care of us. We made bread and everything. Could we stay in our own house? We don't want to go nowhere. We want to stay together."

Natasha lit another cigarette and walked to the window. "How old are you now, Toughboy?"

"Eleven," he said. He hated to say it. Why couldn't he have been thirteen or sixteen or eighteen? Eleven. A little kid. He looked down at the floor, feeling skinny and short.

"Well," said Natasha, as she gazed out the window. She spoke dreamily, in a faraway voice. Her medicine woman voice, thought Sister. "You're a man now. You took care of your sister and cut the wood and killed a bear. I guess you're all grown-up." And as if she knew what he'd been thinking, she added, "Don't have to be big to be grown-up."

They couldn't believe Natasha had said those things. They stared at her, not knowing what to say.

Natasha turned and looked at them for a minute. "Good people. You come from good people. Strong people." Then she turned again to look out the window. She stared off to the slough, smoking, for what seemed to Toughboy and Sister a very long time. They were afraid to move.

Natasha smiled at the slough. "I think you'll come and stay with me. No one won't take you away. You'll stay with me." She shook her head, one hard, short nod. And that meant that was the way it'd be because whatever Natasha said was so.

"Oh, good, Toughboy," whispered Sister.

It was funny, but when the boat was all loaded and Mutt was barking at the bow, they hated to leave. Toughboy felt something sad in his chest. Sister's eyes filled with tears, and when she blinked, the tears spilled down her cheeks.

Natasha understood. "You'll come back. When you're big, you'll run the fish wheel like your dad, and you'll have a smokehouse full of fish."

She started the kicker, and they watched as the camp got smaller and smaller. And when they got around the bend, they couldn't see it anymore.